The LION and *The* UNICORN

AND OTHER HAIRY TALES

Written and Illustrated by

JANE RAY

BOXER BOOKS

First published in
North America in 2015 by Boxer Books Limited.
www.boxerbooks.com

Boxer® is a registered trademark of Boxer Books Limited
Text and illustrations copyright © 2015 Jane Ray

The right of Jane Ray to be identified as the author and
illustrator of this work has been asserted by her
in accordance with the Copyright, Designs and Patents Act, 1988.

The illustrations were prepared using Scraperboard, where the line is etched
onto a thin layer of white china clay on board coated with black India ink.
The text is set in Garamond.

ISBN 978-1-910126-38-7

1 3 5 7 9 10 8 6 4 2

Printed in China

All of our papers are sourced from
managed forests and renewable resources.

For Ros Asquith

CONTENTS

INTRODUCTION

A love of stories is a universal thing. Every film, song, soap opera, and joke is a story with a beginning, a middle, and an end.

To want to know "what happens next" is almost as instinctive as breathing. And it comes naturally to me to collect stories from far and wide – stories that I've read, or overheard, or been told.

Even though I've gathered together two previous collections (*The Emperor's Nightingale and Other Feathery Tales* and *The Little Mermaid and Other Fishy Tales*), which I hope you have enjoyed, there are still plenty more stories and poems in my head, and so I have put this third selection together for you.

This time I have ventured into the forests and jungles, mountains and woods, to find stories about animals of all kinds – growling, snorting, spotted and striped, hairy and scaly, with teeth and claws.

I have always loved animals. I love the variety of creatures on the earth – rough-skinned elephants with their sinuous trunks, yellow-eyed tigers, hulking great bears, elegant springing antelope.

I am moved by the intelligent expressions of gorillas, chimpanzees, dogs, and cats. They have no artifice, no social "face" to present to the world – they just are who they are. They inspire me in my work and enhance my life. My family and I share our home with an elderly cat who is gentle and affectionate, a silent witness to our lives, gloriously indifferent to family drama, but always there – a constant and comforting presence.

Humankind has a paradoxical and confused relationship with animals. They delight and inspire us and yet we use and abuse them. We worship some animals and ill-treat others. We hunt them to extinction and then do our best to conserve them. We sentimentalize them and interpret their behavior in human terms and yet with a stunning lack of humanity, we often drive them out of their natural habitats through the development of ours.

We don't seem to have understood that all of us, human and animal, have a place

in the ecosystem, that we are all linked, that we need each other.

All the stories in this book have something to say about our relationships with animals, and probably reveal more about us than about them. Humans have a natural tendency to anthropomorphize – a long word that means we like to give animals human characteristics. I think we do this in our on-going attempt to make sense of the world, to have a place for everything, to impose human order. By anthropomorphizing, we are trying to understand what animals think and feel and to fit them into our view of the world.

So we talk about the noble lion, the sinister snake, and the mischievous monkey. The camel we see as aloof and the cow as patient and gentle. Our language is peppered with references to them: "as strong as an ox," "like a bull in a china shop," "cunning as a fox."

Some of these characteristics may be based in reality, but generally they are entirely our own invention. The only thing that really holds sway in the natural world is the circle of life and the food chain. Sentiment and imagination and love are human characteristics.

These stories come from all around the world: some are ancient, some more recent; some will be familiar, others I hope may be new to you. There are stories of transformation, of magic and empathy, kindness and trickery. Like a latter day Noah I have herded them together from all over the world — from Africa and India, from America, Greece and the Arctic. We have bears, foxes and wolves, an elephant and a rhinoceros, a leopard and a lion. I have included some mythical creatures too: the terrifying Minotaur and the mysterious unicorn, as well as a cowardly dragon.

I hope you will enjoy them – and if you do, pass them on – tell them again!

BRER WOLF TRIES TO CATCH BRER RABBIT

This story is taken from a collection of wonderful trickster tales that are a huge part of American folklore. Called The Uncle Remus Stories, *many versions were carried to the Caribbean and to America's southern states by African slaves. Brer Rabbit is often the trickster who drives all the other animals to distraction. I chose this story because the wolf, so often the "big bad wolf" in fairy tales, is outwitted by such a small furry creature.*

One fine spring morning, Brer Fox was trotting down the road with his head full of ideas about how to catch Brer Rabbit. This is how he spent most of his waking hours – and most of his dreams too.

He was so caught up in his plans and imaginings that he didn't see Brer Wolf coming toward him until he bumped right into him.

"Cousin Fox," cried Brer Wolf, "look where you're going! You walked right into me!"

"I'm sorry, Cousin Wolf," said the fox, "but you know what I was thinking about, don't you?"

"How to catch Brer Rabbit? You're obsessed with that creature. You've been

trying to catch him all the time I've
known you and that is a mighty long
time," said Brer Wolf.

"I know, I know!" groaned Brer Fox.
"Don't remind me! I have never known
such a wily, sneaky animal in all my life!"

"How can it be," asked Brer Wolf, "that two such impressive characters as we two, feared by one and all, can be outwitted time and time again by a pesky, scrawny, skinny little rabbit? It's demeaning, Brer Fox, that's what it is. BUT – I have the perfect idea to bring an end to this situation and put that rabbit in the pot where he belongs!"

Brer Fox sat down in the road and gave Brer Wolf his full attention. "What is your plan?" he asked. "It had better be good ..."

"Oh it is, it is," laughed Brer Wolf. "This is what we'll do. First of all, you have to persuade Brer Rabbit to come to your house."

"Well, let me stop you right there, my friend," said Brer Fox. "He wouldn't come to my house for anything, not even if you promised him free carrots for a year!"

"So, what you have to do is go home and get into bed, and act like you are dead as dead can be. Lie on your back, with your paws crossed just so, and your fine bushy tail laid out straight. And don't you make one sound, not a squeak mind, until Brer Rabbit comes round to pay his respects to the dear departed. Then, when he's standing over you, weeping and wailing and pretending to mind that you've died, you grab him round his miserable scrawny neck and shove him in the pot over the fire and

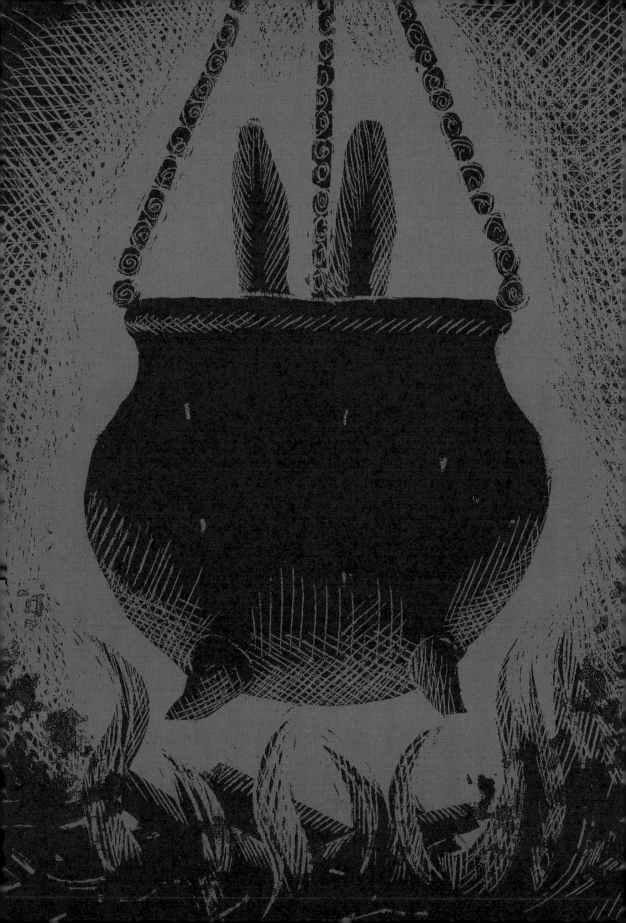

bang down the lid, quick as quick."

"Great idea!" said Brer Fox. "That's bound to work! Good thinking, Brer Wolf! Do you know, I can smell that rabbit stew already? And it smells just fine!!"

So Brer Fox raced home, as fast as he could, to pretend to be dead, and Brer Wolf raced off to Brer Rabbit's house to tell him the sad news.

Brer Wolf knocked hard on Brer Rabbit's door.

No reply.

He shouted through the letterbox, "Brer Rabbit? This is Brer Wolf. I've got something really important to tell you."

Still no reply.

"It's bad news, Brer Rabbit, really bad news. But I guess if you're not interested I'll just go and tell Brer Turtle instead."

Brer Rabbit opened the door a crack, and put out one long ear.

"No, no, Brer Wolf. If it's bad news I want to be the first to know. Go on, tell me ..."

A tear ran down Brer Wolf's face and he dabbed at his eyes with a red-and-white spotted handkerchief. "Our dear friend, Brer Fox, died this morning," he said, and blew his nose loudly.

"Really?" asked Brer Rabbit suspiciously.

"Oh yes," said Brer Wolf. "He never quite recovered from that time you dropped a brick on his head – never was

his own self after that." He shook his head mournfully. "Well, I'll be on my way. I just thought I had to stop by and tell you, seeing as how you and dear dead Cousin Fox had known each other so very long ..."

Brer Rabbit was trying not to smile. "This is very sad news indeed, Brer Wolf. Thank you so much for letting me be the very first to hear it. As you say, Brer Fox and I go back a very long way. Life certainly won't be the same without him."

"It's the least I could do," wept Brer Wolf, sobbing into his handkerchief. "Now I must go and organize Brer Fox's funeral."

No sooner had Brer Wolf gone than

Brer Rabbit raced straight round to Brer
Fox's house.

He peered through the window. Sure
enough, there was Brer Fox laid out on
the bed, in his Sunday best suit, with

his paws folded across his chest and his bushy tail smoothed out straight.

"Poor Brer Fox," sniffed Brer Rabbit. "He certainly looks dead to me. Mind you, everyone knows that when someone dies and a visitor comes to pay their last respects, truly dead people raise a leg in the air and shout 'Wahoo!!'"

Brer Fox raised one leg and shouted
"Wahoo!!" at the top of his voice to show
just how very dead he was.

And Brer Rabbit was off down the
road as fast as his skinny little legs
would carry him!

THE SINGING RINGING TREE

A tree with leaves of tinkling glass is a recurring image in ancient Slavic folklore, and this story was first written down in 1801 in Germany. When I was young I saw a children's film on TV based on that folktale, performed in German with English dubbed over the top.

This story imprinted itself on my mind and stayed with me into adulthood. It surprised me to find that it had rarely been reproduced as a children's book.

There was once a beautiful princess who had shining black hair that rippled down her back in waves, smooth brown skin, and eyes as dark as the night sky. Poems were written to honor her beauty, and birds would stop singing in astonishment as she walked past. Just about everyone who met her fell instantly in love.

But all this attention had made the princess very proud and selfish. She had become quite bored by all the adoration and took it for granted that everyone wanted to marry her. She had lost count of the offers of marriage she had received and had turned them all down.

There was one prince, though, who wouldn't give up. He was so sure he loved the princess, and that he couldn't possibly live without her, that he decided to risk her scorn and ask again.

He brought her a gift of pearls, which everyone knows are made from the tears of mermaids and are very rare indeed, for mermaids hardly ever cry. But the princess looked down her nose at them.

"I already have pearls," she said. "Bring me the Singing Ringing Tree – then I might think about marrying you."

The prince sighed. He knew about the Singing Ringing Tree, a magical tree with leaves of glass that rang with music for those with true love in their hearts. And he knew how much hardship he must go through to find it and bring it back for the princess.

But find it he would, without question. He bowed low to the princess, who sniffed and turned her back on him.

The prince saddled his horse and set off immediately, traveling west.

He rode for three days and three nights,
through a dark forest and across a barren
plain, where a chill wind blew endlessly.
Beyond the plain was a place of bleak
mountains and bare thorn trees.
The prince dismounted and led his horse
through a sort of gateway in the rocks
and down a shingly path.

And then, quite suddenly, there it was:
the Singing Ringing Tree. It stood in a
shaft of sunlight, which made its glass
leaves sparkle, a thing of beauty against
the craggy rocks.

The prince was delighted – his quest
hadn't been as difficult as he had feared it
would be. He ran toward the tree and at
his approach it began to tinkle and sing

in response to
the love in his
heart.

But before
he could touch
it, a creature
appeared from
nowhere,
dancing around
the prince's legs.
It was an evil
little goblin,
covered all over
with coarse
rough hair, and
it had hooves
instead of feet.

His yellow eyes flashed with spite and anger and he shouted at the prince, "Stop right there! That tree is mine and no one shall have it! This is my kingdom and everything in it belongs to me!"

The goblin came closer and thrust his face up at the prince. "I know why you've come," he said in a mocking voice. "You've fallen in love and your princess wants the Singing Ringing Tree."

The prince nodded. "And if you saw her, you would understand," he said. "She is the most beautiful girl I have ever seen."

The goblin smiled a mean little smile and put his hand mockingly on his heart. "I could never resist a love story," he said.

"You may take the tree, my friend."

"Thank you so much," said the prince. "Please let me reward you for your generosity."

"Oh I will, I will!" said the goblin, laughing to himself. "You may take the tree – but there is one condition. If your beautiful princess should fail to fall in love with you, then I will transform you both into whatever form I choose, and you will be compelled to return here to spend the rest of your days under my spell!"

Well, the prince wanted to marry the princess very much and, rather foolishly, he was sure that now he had the Singing Ringing Tree she was bound to fall in

love with him. So he gave the goblin his
word. He took the little tree and tied it
securely to his horse's saddle.

The prince set out once again on

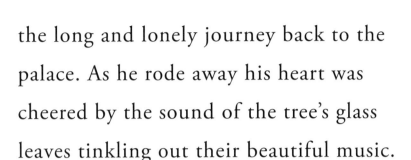

the long and lonely journey back to the palace. As he rode away his heart was cheered by the sound of the tree's glass leaves tinkling out their beautiful music.

After three days and nights of travel he knelt before the princess, amazed once again at how beautiful she was, and presented her with the Singing Ringing Tree.

The princess grabbed it from him without a word of thanks. Now that she had her heart's desire, she had quite forgotten that the prince wanted to marry her.

She ran out into the palace gardens. There was a pool with a fountain just below her bedroom window, and she

immediately gave orders that the royal
gardener should fill in the fountain with
earth from the garden, and plant the tree
there, where she could hear it sing.

"But Your Highness," said the
gardener, "what about the fish in the
pool?"

"Oh, I don't care about them," said
the princess.

And so, the Singing Ringing Tree
was put in place. The sunlight sparkled
on its glassy leaves – but it was
completely silent.

The prince was bowed down with grief.
The princess did not love him. What a
fool he had been to fall so completely in

love with someone who had no thought
or feeling for anything other than
herself. Already he could feel the evil
little goblin's spell flowing through him,
drawing him back to the thorny rocky

kingdom. He lay down at the foot of
the silent Singing Ringing Tree and fell
into a troubled sleep, full of wild and
frightening dreams.

He awoke, in the early morning,
feeling very strange indeed. He opened
his eyes and saw that the arm he was
resting his head on was covered in rough
fur, and ended with great curved black

claws. He tried to get to his feet, but his body was far heavier than it had ever felt before and he fell down onto all fours. He walked like this, toward the palace, lumbering heavily from side to side.

The soldiers, guarding the palace doors, jumped to attention, pointing their spears at him, panic in their eyes. The prince was confused and opened his mouth to speak, "Don't be afraid – it's me – the prince who brought the Singing Ringing Tree!" But the sound that came from his throat was a great deep rumbling growl.

The goblin's wicked magic had transformed the prince from a man to a great bear!

As he stood in the gardens, the
soldiers nervously backing away from
him to the safety of the palace, he heard
a terrible screaming and wailing coming
from the princess's bedroom window.
All at once she came running out into
the garden, distraught. Even through his

bear eyes, the prince could see that she wasn't quite the girl she had been the night before. Her smooth brown skin was coarse and grey in the morning sunlight, and her glossy black hair was tangled and straggly. She fell to her knees and covered her face with dry, scaly hands.

The bear prince went to the princess's side, wanting to calm her, for he knew straight away that her transformation too was the work of the evil little goblin. He spoke quietly into her ear, his voice low and growling, but gentle. "We have to go, princess. Come with me."

The princess had no idea what was happening to her but she felt she couldn't possibly stay at the palace, looking as

she did. She might as well go with this
great hairy bear. She climbed on his back
and buried her face in his fur. Together,
the bear prince and the princess rode off
through the palace gates and west toward
the goblin's kingdom.

After three days and three nights the
bear prince and the princess arrived
and were greeted by the cackles of the

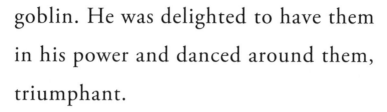

goblin. He was delighted to have them in his power and danced around them, triumphant.

The princess was overwhelmed with misery at the loss of her beauty. She thought it was the only thing she had and without it nothing else mattered. She lay in a cave on the stony ground and wept.

The bear tried his best to comfort her but to no avail. He made her a bed of soft green moss and brought her nuts and sweet honey and berries to eat. At night he lay down outside the cave to keep the princess safe.

Gradually, through her wretchedness, the princess began to notice his kindness. She saw how the birds came to him and perched on his great shaggy head, and how even the most timid of creatures, the deer and the rabbit and the lizard, seemed to trust him.

She began to think less about her own misery. There were no golden mirrors to remind her of her ruined beauty and it began to matter less and less.

She began to help the bear collect food for them both. One day, while she was collecting berries, she came upon a unicorn, caught in a thorn bush. The beautiful creature was stuck fast, its white coat torn and bleeding. The princess gently stroked its head and pulled away the brambles. She tore strips of silk from her dress and bound its wounds.

The evil little goblin, watching this scene from behind a rock, was enraged. He knew that if the princess's heart were to become warmed with love she would no longer be in his power. And if she began to love the bear, then he too would be free of the goblin's enchantment.

The goblin muttered a spell beneath his breath, a cold wicked spell to freeze the ground and put the ice back in her heart.

The stream that ran past the cave where the princess sheltered immediately froze over. With horror she saw that a beautiful silver fish was trapped in the ice. Without hesitation, she took off one of her bejeweled shoes, walked across the

frozen stream and broke the ice around the fish so that it could swim free.

The goblin was furious. He stamped his hooves on the frosty ground and at once the cave collapsed in a heap.

The princess cried out in horror and ran toward the cave. Her first thought was for the bear and she was terrified that he might be hurt. With a pang she realized that she loved him and that she must find him as soon as possible. She couldn't see him in the collapsed cave, but she knew she must find him and be with him.

The goblin was horrified – he could see what was unfolding before his wicked yellow eyes and was determined to stop it.

Again he stamped his hoof and a great
torrent of water came gushing from the
earth, flooding the ground and washing
the princess away in a great wave. Just as
it seemed certain that she would drown,
she was suddenly lifted up and carried to
safety by the great silver fish.

The goblin screamed in rage and
frustration. Again he struck the ground
with his hoof and a great ring of flame
leapt up around the princess. But at the
very same moment the magical unicorn
appeared by her side. The princess
climbed onto the unicorn's back and
they soared up and over the flames to
where the bear stood, outside the ring.
The unicorn dropped the princess at the

bear's feet and the princess flung her arms around him.

"Dear Bear," she cried, "thank goodness you are safe! I love you so much!"

And with that, the fire died down, the waters rolled away, and the frozen ground became covered with soft grass and spring flowers. With a terrible cry of fury the goblin was swallowed up by the earth.

The princess realized that the great furry beast she was holding in her arms was the young prince who wanted to marry her, and he looked into her face, far lovelier than before because it was soft with love.

The spell was broken.

The two lovers made their way slowly

back to the palace. With no horse or evil enchantment to carry them it took far longer than three days and nights, and by the time they reached the palace they had planned their wedding, and named all the children they intended to have.

And, as they walked through the gates of the palace, the air was filled with the music of the Singing Ringing Tree.

THE HEAVENLY
ELEPHANT

*T*his *Indian story follows in the tradition of many folktales where the moral is a light-hearted warning against greed and foolishness: the most famous of these is probably* The Goose that Laid the Golden Egg, *a fable by Aesop. I loved the idea of the great elephant crashing down through the trees, and lumbering around the garden in the moonlight.*

Jasmine worked in the Raja's beautiful garden and had the greenest fingers in the whole of India. At her touch the tiniest seeds and the weediest plants blossomed and flourished. She loved her job and worked hard from dawn until dusk, growing the most colorful flowers and succulent fruit.

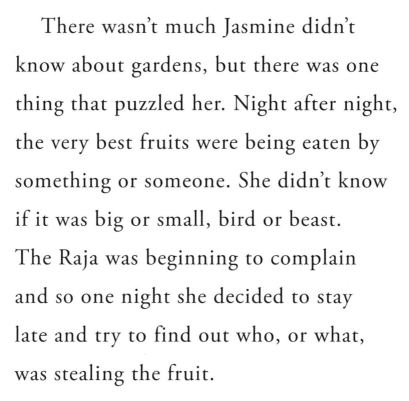

There wasn't much Jasmine didn't
know about gardens, but there was one
thing that puzzled her. Night after night,
the very best fruits were being eaten by
something or someone. She didn't know
if it was big or small, bird or beast.
The Raja was beginning to complain
and so one night she decided to stay
late and try to find out who, or what,
was stealing the fruit.

As the light began to fade she hid
behind a lotus tree and settled down to
wait. The hours passed. The moon rose.
The garden was full of mysterious sounds
– scamperings in the undergrowth and
rustlings in the treetops. Jasmine was
tired and hungry, and just a little bit

scared. She wanted to go home to her brothers and sisters, and her auntie and her grandpapa, but still she kept watch.

Her head was just beginning to nod, when suddenly the peace of the night was shattered by an ear-splitting crash. Jasmine jumped awake and peered out nervously from behind the tree.

An enormous elephant had fallen from the heavens and landed in the moonlit garden! Jasmine watched, amazed, as the mighty creature roamed around, happily picking the tenderest shoots and the ripest fruit from the trees with his long gray trunk. Despite its great size, the elephant moved delicately and carefully and the garden was not damaged at all.

Eventually, when the elephant had eaten enough, he looked up into the night sky and prepared to leave. Quick as lightning, and without really thinking, Jasmine grabbed hold of his tail and hung on as the elephant soared upward toward the

stars. Up and up they flew, rushing
through the inky night sky, the wind
whistling in Jasmine's ears and her hair
streaming behind her. The elephant had
no idea she was there, hitching a ride –
she was a skinny little thing and light
as a feather.

Jasmine clung on for dear life, her eyes tightly shut. After what seemed an age, they slowed and she opened one eye. They passed the seventieth star and beyond she saw great billowing clouds, bathed in a glorious pink light. It looked like heaven!

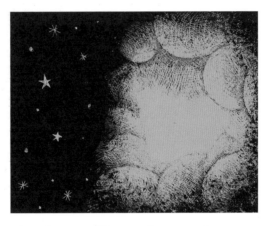

The elephant flew through a great archway in the clouds and landed with a gentle bump. Jasmine let go of the elephant's tail and gazed around her, open-mouthed with astonishment.

They had arrived in another garden – but this one was very different from the one belonging to the Raja. Everything here was made of silver and gold, of precious jewels and glittering gems. And everything was huge, much bigger than on earth.

Great silver trees dripped with huge mangos made of amber. There were golden oranges the size of ostrich eggs and big crystal roses that sparkled like frost.

The elephant still seemed not to notice Jasmine and lay down under the golden boughs of a cherry tree hung with ruby fruit

to sleep off his meal from the Raja's
garden on earth.

Jasmine wandered around the garden.
She reached up to pick a plum, the size
of her hand, but when she tried to bite it,
she realized that it was made of amethyst,
and not a sweet juicy fruit at all. Truly
this was an astonishing and magical
place, but Jasmine
could quite see why
the elephant would
prefer the fruit in
the Raja's garden.
But think how
wealthy she could
be if she took some
of these jewels back

to her family! She didn't earn much for all her hard work in the Raja's garden and she had four little brothers and sisters to keep. And there was Auntie Ameena with her bad back, and Grandpapa Imran with his weakening sight – just think how much better life could be if she filled her pockets with a few of these precious jewels!

She ran around the garden picking
emerald grapes and sapphire blueberries,
and a great golden pomegranate stuffed
with ruby seeds.

At sunset the elephant lumbered to his feet once more, and flew back to the Raja's garden with Jasmine clinging to his tail.

As soon as they landed Jasmine ran home to her family. They were worried because they hadn't seen her since the previous morning, but when she showed them the precious fruits they did a dance all around the kitchen!

"Where did you get these?" asked Hassan.

"Are there any more?" asked Bashir.

"Will you go again?" asked Naimah.

"Can I come with you?" asked Shabina.

"All right! All right!" laughed Jasmine. "I'll take you tonight, but you mustn't breathe a word of this to anyone – it must be our secret!"

They all promised not to tell, but later that evening when Hassan went to fetch water from the well he saw his best friend Ajit. "It won't hurt to tell Ajit," thought Hassan. "After all, he is my very best friend …"

So, swearing him to secrecy he whispered the whole story into Ajit's ear. Well, Ajit could scarcely believe it. He was so astonished by Hassan's story that he went straight home and told his mother, who told Mrs. Aziz, her neighbor, who told her cousin, Bakool.

And before very long, everybody in the town had heard about the Mighty Elephant and the Jeweled Gardens of Heaven.

At sunset, there they all were, standing at the Raja's garden gate, chattering excitedly about what they had heard, about the huge emeralds and diamonds, the enormous garnets and sapphires, and demanding to be taken to the magical gardens.

They wouldn't go away and poor Jasmine had no choice but to agree that they could all go with the elephant when he returned to the Jeweled Gardens of Heaven.

With great difficulty, they all hid themselves in the bushes and behind the trees of the Raja's garden until, with a great crash, the heavenly elephant landed once again by the mango tree.

Everyone watched in awe as he delicately roamed around the garden plucking bananas and apples, pears and oranges. When he had eaten his fill of fruit and was about to leave, Jasmine grabbed hold of his tail. Hassan grabbed Jasmine's hand, who took Bashir's, who

grabbed Auntie Ameena's. Auntie Ameena
held on tightly to Deepak, who held on
to cousin Bakool, who held firmly on
to little Kali. They all held tight as the
Heavenly Elephant took off and climbed
higher and higher into the deep blue sky.
He appeared not to notice the great trail
of people behind him.

He climbed further and further away
from the Raja's garden, closer and closer
to heaven.

He had just passed the seventieth
star when Cousin Bakool whispered
to Deepak, "Tell me again how big
the golden oranges are in the heavenly
garden?" Deepak couldn't remember so
he asked Auntie Ameena. She in turn

asked Bashir, who asked Hassan.

"Jasmine," whispered Hassan, "how
big did you say the golden oranges are?"

"Wait and see," said Jasmine. "We'll be
there soon and you can see for yourself."

But Cousin Bakool couldn't wait. "Tell
me now!" he said.

"They are as big as ostrich eggs,"
said Jasmine.

But Cousin Bakool had never seen
an ostrich egg. "How big is that?" he
called up the line, to where Jasmine
was concentrating on holding on to the
elephant's tail.

Exasperated, Jasmine said, "They are
about this big!" and she held out both
hands to show the size of the golden

oranges, letting go of
the elephant's tail.

    And she and
Hassan and Bashir,
Auntie Ameena,
Deepak, Cousin
Bakool and little
Kali, and all the other
friends and relations
and neighbors,
tumbled head over
heels and back down
to Earth and they
never did get to see
the Jeweled Gardens
of Heaven.

THE LION AND THE UNICORN

This is a traditional English nursery rhyme. I always liked the idea of the real Lion and the mythical Unicorn being linked — it suggests something of Earth and heaven — the grounded and the celestial. When I started researching this book, I discovered that the Lion stands for England and the Unicorn represents Scotland. In 1603 the two symbols were combined in the Royal Coat of Arms of the United Kingdom to symbolize the joining of the two countries.

The lion and the unicorn
Were fighting for the crown
The lion beat the unicorn
All around the town.
Some gave them white bread,
And some gave them brown;
Some gave them plum cake
and drummed them out of town.

THESEUS AND THE MINOTAUR

In this famous Greek myth, the Minotaur is not a real beast, but a terrible combination of bull and man. The idea of this creature entombed and trapped in the middle of the impenetrable Labyrinth maybe taps into our human fear of the beast within each of us, our wild side, buried deep. This horror is contrasted with the triumph of Theseus's determination to overturn entrenched and unquestioning tradition. And so, ultimately, this is an uplifting and inspiring story.

Prepare to enter the Labyrinth!

Deep beneath the royal palace of Crete there was a terrible place – a maze of endless twisting echoing passages, dark as a cave. It was called the Labyrinth and no one who entered it ever found their way out again.

And in its dark heart lived the Minotaur, a brutal beast, half man, half bull, who feasted on human flesh and had never seen the light of day.

King Minos, the ruler of Crete, was a powerful man – he had to be. In order to keep the monstrous Minotaur under control, every year he demanded that seven young women and seven young men from the neighboring country of Athens be sent unarmed into the

Labyrinth to feed the beast. If Aegeus, the Athenian King, refused to hand them over, then King Minos promised he would unleash a dreadful war on them.

And so it was that every year, in springtime, when the air was scented with orange blossom and the doves called in the olive groves, a ship with black sails arrived in the harbor of Athens.

Springtime! When the thoughts of the young should be turning to love, the hearts of the young people of Athens were filled with dread. Fourteen young sons and daughters of Athens were chosen by lot and taken onto the ship, back to Crete. The families they left behind were demented with grief and King Aegeus

could do nothing to help them. He felt
their agony keenly, for he too had a son,
a strong youth called Theseus, whom he
loved with all his heart.

In the year that Theseus was seventeen
years old, on the day that the lots were to
be drawn, everyone was gathered before
the palace. There was a terrible silence
hanging over the citizens of Athens as
they prayed, "Please – don't let it be my
daughter, please don't take my son ..."

Prince Theseus, standing with his
father, suddenly felt a surge of anger.

"Why do we put up with it?" he cried.
"This cannot continue."

Aegeus, his whole body weighed
down with the horror of the situation,

looked gravely at his son. "We have no choice," he said. "The Cretans are far more powerful than we are. They would destroy us all. It is better to sacrifice a few to save the rest."

"Well, in that case," said Theseus, "choose thirteen people. I will be the fourteenth and I will kill the Minotaur!"

The King wept. He begged Theseus

not to go. "You will surely die, my precious son. Please don't go."

But Theseus had all the determination of youth, and Aegeus saw that he would not be dissuaded.

He took him in his arms and said,
"I understand my son, and I am proud
of your bravery. Will you make me one
promise? If the ship returns, and you are
on board, please will you exchange the
black sails of death for white ones?
Then I will know, even from a long way
off, that you are alive."

Theseus promised. Then the ship sailed
slowly out of the harbor, and a great wail
of grief rose from the Athenians.

When the ship arrived in Crete, word
quickly reached King Minos that the
Prince of Athens was on board.

The other thirteen young captives
were led to the palace dungeons but
Theseus was summoned into the King's

presence and invited to take his last meal at the royal table. Minos admired the young man – his was a noble sacrifice.

Theseus wasn't sure that he would have much of an appetite, but his heart was lifted somewhat when he saw that Minos's beautiful daughter Ariadne was joining them.

While Minos and Theseus talked

formally of kingly things, Ariadne looked
in wonder at the handsome young man
on the other side of the table.

"He is much too lovely to be torn to
pieces by the Minotaur," she thought.
"And brave too – a man like this ought
not to die. I have to find a way to help
him escape his awful fate."

As they ate, Ariadne racked her brains. Gradually an idea began to form in her mind. She saw that Theseus had finished his wine and she took the jug and went to his side to refill his glass. "Don't be afraid," she whispered in his ear. "I will not let you die."

Later that night Theseus was locked in the dungeon with the other prisoners, who clung together in fear and dread of what was to come.

King Minos retired to his room and took a sleeping draught, for his guilty conscience would not let him sleep naturally. When Ariadne was sure he was deeply asleep in his bed, she set about her plan.

Picking up a basket, she crept to the palace kitchens. They were quiet for the night, all work done, and it was easy enough to take a flagon of wine and steal back to her bedroom.

Beside her bed was a painted wooden box containing a ball of golden thread. She put it in the basket and crept silently into her father's bedchamber. She took some of the potent sleeping draught and poured it into the flagon of wine. On a carved chest by Minos's bed was a gleaming sword, as sharp as a shark's tooth, which she also laid carefully in the basket.

Ariadne slipped silently through the darkened halls of the great palace and then down some stone steps to the dungeons. When she came to the guards at the dungeon door she smiled and said to them, "My father has sent you some wine as a reward for your vigilance in caring for our prisoners – here – pass the bottle around and drink your fill." The guards were delighted for it was going to be a long night. They thanked the Princess and drank deeply.

Ariadne walked back up the steps and waited for a while. Before long she could hear snoring and knew it was safe to proceed with her plan.

Stealing past the sleeping guards, she took the keys from a hook on the wall and carefully let herself into the prison.

The young Athenians were huddled together in the corner of the dungeon.

Theseus sat alone, trying to work out a way of killing the Minotaur with his bare hands and saving them all.

Ariadne went straight to him.
"I promised I wouldn't let you die – follow me," she said and led him to another door at the back of the prison. They went through it and down a dark tunnel, which seemed to go deeper and deeper underground and finally opened out into a cave. At the back of the cave there was a great metal gate.

This was the entrance to the Labyrinth.

"This is what you must do," said Ariadne. She gave Theseus the ball of golden thread, but tied the end of it around her wrist. "Roll this ball ahead of you through the maze – it will take you to the center where the Minotaur lies. When you reach him, kill him with this sword of my father's. Don't hesitate – be swift and brutal for there will be no second chance. Then when you have killed him you can follow the thread back to me. I will be here."

"The time has come then," thought Theseus. He opened the metal gate and a terrible bellowing roar rang through the twisting passages. He was almost overwhelmed by the great stench that met his nostrils. He dropped the ball of thread on the ground and it began to unroll before him, glowing softly in the gloom.

The ball of thread rolled gently onward, down a slope. It rolled round a corner and on, then a sharp left and right and round again. It seemed to be doubling back on itself and suddenly Theseus came up against a stone wall, a

dead end. He turned back and followed the passageway along. He had totally lost his bearings by now, and the passageways seemed to be getting narrower and darker. The darkness was suffocating.

Fighting a rising sense of panic, Theseus paused and gathered himself. He thought of his fellow captives, clinging together in terror in the dungeon. He thought of his father's despair. And he thought of Ariadne's beautiful face and bright eyes, and his courage returned.

"I will kill this beast," he muttered under his breath.

Another low roar echoed through the Labyrinth, closer now, and Theseus realized, with a sudden clutch of fear,

that he was getting nearer to the center, nearer to the beast.

Around the next corner the sounds changed. He could hear a snorting and a stamping. The smell of the creature was overwhelming – a stink of rotting flesh and hot rancid breath. Every instinct in his body was telling him to turn around, to run back the way he had come, away from this dreadful thing.

"I will kill this beast!" Theseus muttered again.

There was silence, a pause. Theseus crept forward, edging closer and closer. And then quite suddenly the Minotaur was there in front of him, a vast bulky

creature, looming over him, eyes glowing like red coals, head down, ready to charge. Theseus stood his ground until the beast was almost upon him, then he leapt to one side and the Minotaur lumbered into the rocky wall, stunning itself. Shaking its massive head, it turned, but not before Theseus had plunged the sword deep into the creature's thick neck.

With a bellow that almost burst Theseus's eardrums, the Minotaur staggered sideways. It shook its head again, gathering its strength and charged at Theseus. It knocked him to the ground and planted a great foot in his chest. Theseus knew that death was upon him and with both hands he thrust the sword up and straight through the Minotaur's wicked heart. It gave a long, keening howl and staggered back. With a great shuddering exhalation, it collapsed, and died.

There was silence suddenly in the Labyrinth. Theseus struggled to his feet and leaned exhausted against the wall, his breath coming in great ragged gasps.

"It is over," he thought. "It is done. I have killed the beast!"

He recovered his wits and found the end of the golden thread, which he had dropped in the combat. He began to rewind the ball, following the tortuous passages back to Ariadne.

And there she was, as she had promised, with the thirteen young

Athenians on their knees with gratitude to their Prince who had saved them all.

"Follow me – quickly," said Ariadne and she took Theseus's hand.

The guards were still in a stupefied state but beginning to stir. She led the company past them speedily, through the dungeons, up the stairs and out into the soft sunlight of a perfect spring morning.

There, she looked at Theseus and
suddenly had an idea. "Let me come with
you to Athens," she said. She could see
no future for herself in Crete, for her
father had been willing to sacrifice the
sons and daughters of Athens for so many
years, with hardly a thought. It had taken
Theseus's bravery to end the horror.

"But of course," said Theseus.

They boarded the ship, which was
still moored in the harbor, and set sail
for home. It was a wonderful journey,
as you can imagine, full of relief and
celebration. The tale was told over and
over of how Theseus had slaughtered
the Minotaur with Ariadne's help, and
the young men and women who had so

recently cowered in terror were full of song and light and love.

So happy were they that they forgot to replace the terrible black sails on the ship.

Poor King Aegeus, waiting on the cliff top, desperate for his beloved son's safe return, saw the ship on the horizon. As it came closer, he realized that its sails were black, which could mean only one thing – that Theseus, his dear boy, and all the other sons and daughters of Athens, had perished at the hands of the Minotaur. With a great cry of despair, King Aegeus flung himself from the cliff top to the rocks below.

It is a puzzle of life that great happiness and great tragedy can exist side by side. Theseus could not forgive himself that his father never knew the Minotaur was destroyed and that his son was gloriously alive. But eventually he became King of Athens, and by ruling as wisely as his father had before him, he kept something of Aegeus alive.

And he named the great sea into which the old King had flung himself, the Aegean Sea. You can see it still, named on the map, and stretched out beneath the cliffs, sparkling in the sunshine, deep and blue and peaceful.

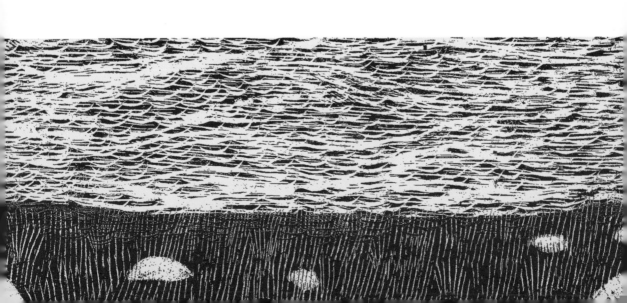

HOW THE RHINOCEROS GOT HIS SKIN

I loved the Just So stories when I was a child – the completely fantastical accounts of how various animals came by their characteristics: "How the Leopard Got His Spots," "How the Elephant Got His Trunk," and more. Written by Rudyard Kipling, who was born in India, they were published in 1902. It was hard to know which story to choose for this collection, as they are all so witty and inventive, but it was the idea of the Rhino slipping out of his suit that made me decide on this one in the end. I hope you enjoy it too!

There was once a man, Best Beloved, an Indian man, who lived by the side of the Red Sea where it is very hot and not much can grow except palm trees. He lived alone and every week he made himself a most delicious cake. For six whole days he looked forward to his treat and on the seventh day he would sit down and eat the whole cake, every crumb, all in one go.

Now, one particular week, the man made an especially wonderful cake. He stirred in butter and eggs, sugar and currants, and every delicious tropical fruit you can think of.

Then he set it to cook on a small stove outside his hut and went off to find the rest of his supper – shellfish and berries and coconuts.

While he was away, a huge rhinoceros came wandering out of the forest and down toward the Red Sea. The huge rhinoceros put his great nose in the air and sniffed. A wonderful smell wafted toward him on the tropical breeze. The rhinoceros never could resist the smell of a cake baking, and he lumbered over to the stove. The cake was rising nicely in its baking tin. It was golden and sprinkled with sugar. The rhinoceros turned his great head, stuck the horn on the top of his nose straight into the cake and ran back into the forest as fast as he could. The man was just walking back up the beach when he saw the great rhinoceros running back into the forest with the beautiful cake on his horn.

"Hey you!" shouted the man, running as fast as he could. "That's my cake! I collected the ingredients, I cooked it, and I'm going to eat it all – every last bit!"

But the rhinoceros just glanced at
the man through his little piggy eyes,
and then he disappeared into the forest.
The man was jumping up and down with
rage and disappointment, shaking his fist
in the air.

"I've looked forward to that cake
the whole week! Come back here AT
ONCE!"

The rhinoceros took absolutely no
notice at all.

The man sat down by the edge of
the water and wept at the loss of his
wonderful cake.

"It would have been such a delicious
cake," he moaned to himself, "for it had
the most golden of eggs, the sweetest

sugar, the creamiest butter and the plumpest currants ..." and he sighed and wept some more.

But gradually his tears began to dry and he stopped sniffing and blew his nose. Then he began to think about revenge.

"I know," he thought, "when the weather gets even hotter than it is now, the rhinoceros will want to come and swim in the Red Sea to cool off. I've seen him many a time. He comes down to the water's edge and he unbuttons his top suit. Then he folds it up neatly and leaves it on the rocks."

For yes indeed, Best Beloved, in those far distant days, the rhinoceros was very

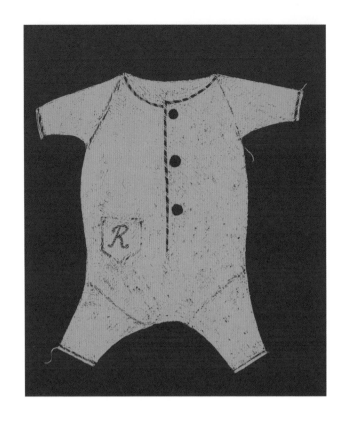

smooth and shiny, and his coat had no creases. And the Indian man knew that the rhinoceros's top coat, or suit, was kept on with three large buttons that buttoned up under his tummy.

The man got down on his hands and knees in front of his hut, and he swept together all the crumbs that had fallen from the cake when the rhinoceros stole it.

Then he sat himself down behind a rock at the water's edge and waited for the rhinoceros to come down for a swim. He waited patiently for several days, until the weather got very hot and, sure enough, along came the rhinoceros. The man watched as he undid his three buttons and slipped off his smooth gray suit and lumbered down into the sea, relaxing in the cool water.

The man slipped out from behind his rock with the bag of cake crumbs in his hand. He crept over to the rhinoceros's suit and shook all the crumbs, which were stale and dry by now, inside, and folded it back up, all neat and tidy. Then he retreated behind the rock and waited.

After a while, the rhinoceros emerged from the sea, feeling refreshed and happy. He climbed into his smooth gray suit and did up the three buttons.

You know what it feels like to get biscuit crumbs in the bed, don't you, Best Beloved, or a little bit of gravel in your sock? Well, it wasn't very long before the prickly, tickly cake crumbs in his clothes began to make the rhinoceros feel very uncomfortable indeed.

He growled and began to roll around on the beach trying to get rid of the scratchy feeling in his suit. He rolled around so much that the three buttons came off. He rubbed up against a palm tree, trying to stop the itchy sensation,

and gradually, his suit began
to get rumpled and crumpled,
and wrinkled and crinkled,
until it was no longer a
smooth, shiny gray suit
but the creased and
wrinkled skin you see
on the rhinoceros
today.

   And that is how
it happened, Best
Beloved – that is
how the rhinoceros
got his skin.

THE TALE
OF CUSTARD
THE DRAGON

Ogden Nash was an American poet. He was well known for his light verse and wrote more than 500 comic poems. I love the rhythm of this story poem, and the wonderful rhymes. It's a great one to read out loud or, even better, to learn by heart!

Belinda lived in a little white house,

With a little black kitten and a little gray mouse,

And a little yellow dog and a little red wagon,

And a realio, trulio, little pet dragon.

Now the name of the little black kitten was Ink,

And the little gray mouse, she called her Blink,

And the little yellow dog was sharp as Mustard,

But the dragon was a coward, and she called him Custard.

Custard the dragon had big sharp teeth,

And spikes on top of him and scales underneath,

Mouth like a fireplace, chimney for a nose,

And realio, trulio, daggers on his toes.

Belinda was as brave as a barrel full of bears,

And Ink and Blink chased lions down the stairs,

Mustard was as brave as a tiger in a rage,

But Custard cried for a nice safe cage.

Belinda tickled him, she tickled him unmerciful,

Ink, Blink and Mustard, they rudely called him Percival,

They all sat laughing in the little red wagon

At the realio, trulio, cowardly dragon.

Belinda giggled till she shook the house,

And Blink said Week!, which is giggling for a mouse,

Ink and Mustard rudely asked his age,

When Custard cried for a nice safe cage.

Suddenly, suddenly they heard a nasty sound,

And Mustard growled, and they all looked around.

Meowch! cried Ink, and Ooh! cried Belinda,

For there was a pirate, climbing in the winda.

Pistol in his left hand, pistol in his right,

And he held in his teeth a cutlass bright,

His beard was black, one leg was wood;

It was clear that the pirate meant no good.

Belinda paled, and she cried, Help! Help!

But Mustard fled with a terrified yelp,

Ink trickled down to the bottom of the household,

And little mouse Blink strategically mouseholed.

But up jumped Custard, snorting like an engine,

Clashed his tail like irons in a dungeon,

With a clatter and a clank and a jangling squirm

He went at the pirate

like a robin at a worm.

The pirate gaped at

Belinda's dragon,

And gulped some

grog from his pocket

flagon,

He fired two bullets

but they didn't hit,

And Custard gobbled

him, every bit.

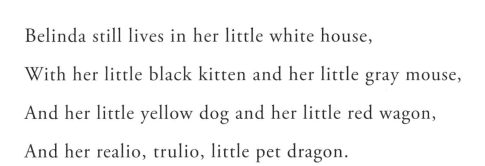

Belinda embraced him, Mustard licked him,

No one mourned for his pirate victim.

Ink and Blink in glee did gyrate

Around the dragon that ate the pyrate.

Belinda still lives in her little white house,

With her little black kitten and her little gray mouse,

And her little yellow dog and her little red wagon,

And her realio, trulio, little pet dragon.

Belinda is as brave as a barrel full of bears,

And Ink and Blink chase lions down the stairs,

Mustard is as brave as a tiger in a rage,

But Custard keeps crying for a nice safe cage.

– Ogden Nash

THE OLD LADY
AND HER SON

*T*his story is an Inuit tale from the Arctic.
I was drawn to it because I like stories
that have an element of "the circle of life."
They take away the fear and dread of
death and put it in its proper context — as
a natural part of the shape and pattern of
life. And the love between the old woman
and the beautiful, fearsome wild creature
that she comes to see as her son is moving
and tender.

Way, way North, as far North as you
can possibly go, where the world is white
with snow and ice from one year's end to
the next, there lived an old woman.

Her name was Kesuk and she was all
alone in the world. But although she
had no husband or children to hunt
for her, and she was too old to hunt for

herself, she never went hungry. She lived in a village where everyone looked after each other, and her neighbors made sure she always had food. When they went hunting they would bring Kesuk a piece of whale meat, or seal, or blubber.

But though her stomach was full enough, her heart sometimes ached with loneliness for there was no one to wake up with as each day dawned, or to tell stories to as night fell. Even though her neighbors were kind, she still sometimes wished for someone of her own to sit by the fire with.

One day when the men of the village went out hunting, they found a little bear cub, curled up and frozen in the snow. "His mother must have abandoned him," the hunters decided, "or been killed by another village. Her poor cub has frozen to death."

They carried the cub back to the village and took it to the old woman.

"We've brought this for you," they said. "There's lots of meat on it and it will keep you fed for days."

Kesuk was delighted and took the bear cub into her house to thaw it ready for cooking.

But as the little bear grew warmer, Kesuk noticed that it was moving – not dead at all!

She moved him closer to the fire and fed him tenderly with whale milk and seal blubber. As the bear gradually recovered he nuzzled up to the old woman and fell asleep. Kesuk whispered in his snowy white ear: "Since you have no mother and I have no son, we shall be everything to each other," she said.

"I will be your mother and you will be my child, and we shall do very nicely."

As the days and weeks went by, the little bear learned how to hunt, both by watching the human hunters, and through instinct, for every bear can hunt – it is only natural. Kesuk grew quite plump from all the food the bear caught for her, and she was soon able to repay the kindness of her neighbors, for the bear caught more than the two of them could eat.

Kesuk called the little bear K'eyush, which means Bear Cub in the language of the Inuit people.

K'eyush loved to roll in the snow and chase the birds. The children from the village soon joined him, clambering on his back for rides and playing tag.

But as K'eyush grew bigger, and became better and better at hunting, the men of the village began to feel jealous of him. "That bear makes us look useless," they grumbled. "He'll catch so much fish and meat there won't be enough for all of us and our families will go hungry."

And the women began to mutter to each other. "He's getting bigger and bigger – he might play with our children nicely now, but what will happen when he is fully grown? One day he'll realize that the children aren't his playmates but his prey!"

The villagers met together. They decided that they must kill K'eyush.

The children, overhearing their parents' plan, were horrified. They ran to Kesuk and her bear son.

"Run away, K'eyush!" they cried. "The men are going to kill you! Run away now!"

Kesuk confronted the villagers. "Please, I beg you – do not kill my son. He hunts for me and I share the food with your wives. He plays with the children – he does no harm! I will be so sad and lonely if he goes – he protects me like a son."

But her neighbors were determined. They shouted at her, "Kesuk – you know what will happen if we have a fully grown bear in our midst – it cannot be!

No – we will kill him and his meat will
feed us and his fur will keep us warm.
Go home, Kesuk, and don't interfere with
what has to be done!"

Kesuk, horrified, stumbled home and put her arms around K'eyush's neck, holding her face against his.

Suddenly, there was a great knocking at her door and she was filled with fear, but it was only the village children, crowding into her little home.

"We have an idea, Kesuk," they said. "If K'eyush leaves the village and returns to the wild, the grown-ups won't need to kill him – no one will fear him hurting us if he is back with his own kind."

"But I will never see him again," wept Kesuk. "He will grow to adulthood and I won't recognize him from all the other bears."

But the children had the answer to

that too. They went to the fire and mixed
soot with some whale blubber to make
a greasy black paint. Then they smeared
a little of it on K'eyush's side, a black
streak against his white fur. They said,
"Now, even though K'eyush has to leave
the village he has a special mark and we
will always know our friend.

We will make our fathers promise never to
kill the bear with the black mark."

Kesuk knew this was the best plan, but
her poor heart was breaking. "I will always
love you, my dearest son," wept Kesuk,
"but I fear you will soon forget all about
me and the happiness we have shared. But
go now, go back to your real home."

K'eyush seemed to understand.
He sniffed at her one last time and rubbed
his face against hers. Then he trudged
away, across the icy wastes. Just once he
stopped and turned to look at her – and
then he was gone.

Kesuk missed her son terribly and wept
great tears that froze on her wrinkled cheeks.

Time passed, as time does.

One morning she woke very early after a
night full of dreams of K'eyush.

Before the rest of the village was
awake, she went outside and called softly
across the ice: "K'eyush, my wonderful
son, I long to see you again. Please come
to me."

All was silence in the early light, and
Kesuk bowed her head against the cold.

But when she looked up, there was a great white bear coming toward her.

"My son, is it you?" she whispered. The bear came closer and the old woman wondered if it might eat her. But as he drew near, she saw the black smudge along his side and she held out her arms.

K'eyush dropped a pile of freshly caught fish at her feet and rested his great head against her shoulder. With tears in her eyes, Kesuk stroked his silky white ears.

Then, in silent understanding of what must be, she picked up the fish and returned to the village, and K'eyush retreated into the icy wastes.

But from then on, they met each

morning at dawn and the Polar Bear Son never failed to bring food to his mother.

The years went on and Kesuk grew older and more frail, and the day came when she realized that her time on Earth was drawing to a close. As the first pale light of dawn colored the sky pink, she crept from her house and crossed the ice to where K'eyush was waiting for her. She put her arms around his neck, burying her face in his soft white fur, and took her last breath.

K'eyush carried Kesuk back to the village, and laid her gently in the snow, keeping watch over his mother until the villagers came.

THE LEOPARD'S PROMISE

This story has its roots in many tales from Africa and India.

It is a 'trickster' tale, which I wrote myself, where a smaller, weaker animal triumphs over a mighty creature through wits and cunning rather than through physical power. Here, the clever jackal tricks the splendid but arrogant leopard by pretending that he doesn't understand.

One day, a man was strolling through the forest, humming softly to himself. The sun was shining and the birds were singing and all was well with the world. Quite suddenly, though, he came upon a cage set among the trees and in the cage was a big, beautiful leopard.

"Good afternoon," called the leopard, in her most charming voice. "I don't

suppose I could bother you to just unlock this cage door and let me out?"

The man looked at the leopard's rippling muscles, glistening teeth, and ferocious claws.

"I think not, my friend," he said. "If I let you out you'd just eat me without a second thought!"

"But why on earth would I do that?" purred the leopard. "If you were to free me from this cage I would be eternally in your debt – I promise I won't eat you."

The man shook his head, for he was no fool, and began to walk on. But the leopard started to weep. She sobbed great sorrowful sobs and tears trickled down her golden fur. The man couldn't bear to see such a beautiful and majestic creature so distraught.

"All right, all right," he said. "I'll let you out. But remember that you have promised you won't eat me."
He opened the cage door and the leopard sprang out and crouched before him snarling.

"Thank you very much," she said, a cruel smile curling around her mouth. "And just in time for dinner!"

"B-but that's not fair!" stammered the man. "You promised!"

"Did I mention anything about 'fair'?" snarled the leopard.

She crept closer to the man, who had fallen to his knees, wringing his hands and shaking like a leaf.

The leopard was enjoying her power and thought she'd have a little game with the man before she devoured him.

"I'll tell you what we'll do," said the leopard. "In return for letting me out of the cage, which I admit was a very kind thing to do, thank you so much, I will let you ask the first three living things that you see if they think it's fair for me to eat you. If they say it's not, then I will let you go. But if they think it is fair, I will have you for dinner! What do you think?"

"Well, at least this plan buys me some time," thought the man, and he agreed. He looked around for someone to ask, but there were no animals or people nearby, just the trees and the river.

So the man went up to an ancient and wise-looking tree. He looked up into its great spreading branches. "Dear wise tree," he said. "This leopard was trapped in a cage and I very kindly set her free. Do you think it's fair if she now eats me?"

The tree rustled its leaves. "Well," it said, "what is 'fair'? Is it fair that I give you humans shelter and fruit, and shade from the sun, but in return you tear off my branches to feed your cattle and chop me down to build your houses? What will be will be, my friend – 'fair' doesn't come into it."

The leopard licked her lips.

The man was getting very anxious now. He ran to the river and looked deep into its fast flowing waters. "Dear wise river," he said. "This leopard was locked in a cage and I very kindly let her out. Do you think it's fair if she now eats me?"

But the river replied, "Well now, what is 'fair'? Is it fair that I give you fresh clear water to drink and water your crops, and yet in return you wash your dirty clothes in me and empty all your rubbish into me? What will be will be, my friend – and that is just life."

The leopard sharpened her claws.

The man was very worried indeed by now, but just then a jackal came trotting down the road, whistling cheerfully to himself.

"Dear kind jackal," the man said. "Please will you help me?"

"Well, I'll certainly try," said the jackal, "but you know me – I'm not the brightest animal in the forest! You'll have

to explain what you need from me very carefully!"

The man told the jackal the whole story, saying, "Surely you can see, that if I was kind enough to release this leopard from her cage, she really should keep her promise not to eat me?"

"Well now, I'm not too sure," said the jackal. "It seems like a terribly complicated story."

He turned to the leopard. "Can I just get this straight? So the man was in the cage, and you let him out to have him for dinner?"

"No, no, no," said the man, before the leopard could answer. "The leopard was in the cage and I KINDLY let her out, because she promised she wouldn't eat me." "I'm afraid I'm rather confused," said the jackal.

"How on earth did a great big intelligent, brave, noble leopard get into the cage at all? I'm really not sure that I understand exactly what has happened here ..."

The leopard was beginning to get rather impatient with all this waiting around.

"Oh, do hurry up and decide," snarled the leopard, "I'm getting very hungry."

"Yes indeed," said the jackal. "In order to make a judgement, I need to have all the facts. Could you just show me, Leopard, how you got into the cage? Was it through the bars? Or through the door?"

With a roar of irritation the leopard walked back into the cage. "Like this, you stupid creature! Now do you understand?"

"Oh, yes! Thank you so much, dear Leopard!

I understand completely!" said the jackal,
and he slammed the door shut.

"Thank you so much, dear Jackal,"
said the man. "You've saved my life!"

"Well yes, I have, haven't I," said the
jackal. "And perhaps you'll remember
that the next time you chase me out of
your chicken coop!"

And he trotted off down the road.

THE CAMEL

I often find that "facts" like the one in this Ogden Nash poem, which really should be very simple to learn, are actually very confusing ...

The camel has a single hump;

The dromedary, two;

Or else the other way around.

I'm never sure. Are you?

– Ogden Nash

I'M A GNU

I was brought up on this Flanders and Swann song, which was a favorite of my parents, and I can recite the words from memory! It used to make me and my sisters fall off our chairs with laughter. The words are incredibly clever, and I love the fact that something that was remarkably witty in the 1960s still stays fresh and makes us laugh all these years later. It really needs to be read out loud to fully appreciate the absurdity of some of the rules that govern the English language.

A year ago last Thursday I was strolling
    in the zoo,
when I met a man who thought he knew
    the lot.
He was laying down the law about the
    habits of Baboons,
And how many quills a porcupine
    has got.
So I asked him: "What's that
    creature there?"

He answered: "Oh, H'it's a H'elk."

I might of gone on thinking that was true,

If the animal in question hadn't put that
   chap to shame,

And remarked: "I h'aint a H'elk.
   I'm a Gnu!"

"I'm a Gnu, I'm a Gnu

The g-nicest work of g-nature in the zoo

I'm a Gnu, How do you do

You really ought to k-now w-ho's w-ho.

I'm a Gnu, Spelt G-N-U

I'm g-not a Camel or a Kangaroo

So let me introduce,

I'm g-neither man nor moose

Oh g-no g-no g-no
   I'm a Gnu!"

I had taken furnished lodgings down at
    Rustington-on-Sea,
Whence I travelled on to Ashton-under
    Lyne it was actually,
And the second night I stayed there I was
    woken from a dream,
That I'll tell you all about some other time.
Among the hunting trophies on the wall
    above my bed,

Stuffed and mounted, was a face I
   thought I knew;
A Bison? No, it's not a Bison. An Okapi?
   Unlikely, really. A Hartebeest?
When I thought I heard a voice:
   "I'm a Gnu!"

"I'm a Gnu, A g-nother gnu

I wish I could g-nash my

    teeth at you!

I'm a Gnu, How do you do

You really ought to k-now

    w-ho's w-ho.

I'm a Gnu, Spelt G-N-U,

Call me Bison or Okapi

    and I'll sue

G-nor am I the least

Like that dreadful Hartebeest,

Oh, g-no, g-no, g-no,

G-no g-no g-no I'm a Gnu

G-no g-no g-no I'm a Gnu!"

       – Flanders and Swann

Acknowledgments
and sources

Story research by Ann Jungman and Jane Ray.

Brer Wolf – Uncle Remus: His Songs and His Sayings, by Joel Chandler Harris, published by Penguin Classics 1982 (originally published in 1880). Also in *The Classic Tales of Brer Rabbit* by Joel Chandler Harris, David Borgenicht and Don Daily, published by Courage in 2008.

The Singing Ringing Tree – I have based my retelling on the children's film made by East German Studio DEFA in 1957, directed by Francesco Stefani, which was shown on British television as a part of the *Tales From Europe* series in the 1960s, and also on the picture book retelling by Selina Hastings, illustrated by Louise Brierley, which was first published by Walker Books in 1988.

The Heavenly Elephant – This folk tale originates in the Indian State of Bihar, and there are many different retellings, such as one that features a bull instead of an elephant, which I found in *Stories of India*, retold by Anna Milbourne, with illustrations by Linda Edwards and published by Usborne in 2005.

The Lion and the Unicorn – A traditional English nursery rhyme.

Theseus and the Minotaur – This appears in Book VIII of *Ovid's Metamorphoses*. I also looked at *The Usbourne Book of Greek Myths*, published by Usbourne in 2010 (by Anna Milbourne, Louie Stowell, Elena Temporin and Simona Bursi). And *Theseus and the Minotaur* by Hugh Lupton, published by Barefoot Books in 2013.

How the Rhinoceros Got his Skin – From *The Just-So Stories for Little Children* by Rudyard Kipling, first published by Macmillan and Co. in 1902.

The Tale of Custard the Dragon – From *Bed Riddance,* published by Simon and Schuster 1935 &1936, reprinted with kind permission of Curtis Brown, Ltd. NY. Ogden Nash (1902-1971).

The Old Lady and Her Son – This retelling is based on a story from a 1921 collection by Knud Rasmussen, called *Eskimo Folk-Tales*, and also on *The Polar Bear Son: An Inuit Tale* by Lydia Dabcovich, published by Houghton Mifflin Books in 1999.

The Leopard's Promise – Based on a story from Zimbabwe, Africa, retold in *Stories Gogo Told Me* by Lisa Grainger, published by Penguin Books 2007, and "The Trapped Tiger" from *Stories From India*, retold by Anna Milbourne, Usbourne, 2005.

The Camel – From *Bed Riddance,* published by Simon and Schuster 1935 &1936, reprinted with kind permission of Curtis Brown, Ltd. NY. Ogden Nash (1902-1971).